signed
by
Burguières

ONE
CENTIMETER

Grace,
Cheryl Burguières
1999

ONE CENTIMETER

Second Edition

By
CHERYL COURRÉGÉ BURGUIÈRES

ILLUSTRATED BY
GEORGE RODRIGUE

Designed by
Aimée Bernard de Rubio

GULF PUBLISHING COMPANY
HOUSTON, TEXAS

Gulf Publishing Company
Book Division
P.O. Box 2608 · Houston, Texas 77252-2608

10 9 8 7 6 5 4 3 2 1

ISBN 0-87719-368-1
Printed on acid-free paper.

Second Edition
September 1999

For Philip, Emily, and Martial

Their love graces my life.

FOREWORD

"Goal Setting for Writers" was the course Cheryl Burguières had mustered the courage to take — knowing she might be bullied into taking herself seriously as a writer. The brochure for Rice University's School of Continuing Studies warned just that: "Casey Kelly wants to be your personal writing coach." Yipes. It strikes terror in the hearts of many writers — published and unpublished — who sign up. It strikes terror in their instructor, too, as each new group arrives to be challenged for reasons only they know — or don't. It's my job to find out, then push them past their invisible barriers. I worry that I'm up to the task.

On that first night, as I surveyed the room, the petite brunette's enviably large brown eyes seemed to betray one thought: "Please don't call on me!" So I began on the other side of the room, asking others to express their reasons for enrolling — hoping by the time we reached the brunette she would feel more comfortable.

Memory, especially mine, isn't perfect. But I seem to recall asking Cheryl to speak louder. She did, indicating she was "just" writing a memoir of her family history, "just" as an exercise, and that she hadn't really considered writing anything for publication. I challenged that a bit, but Cheryl knew what she wanted. Fine. I secretly wondered if there were a way to help Cheryl get "out there."

One evening, as I described what I call Southern Lady Disease (yes, there's also a Southern Gentleman Disease), I caught a glimmer in Cheryl's big tell-all eyes. They knew what I meant. Southern Lady Disease, a condition I share with her, takes root in young girls as they are trained to become well-bred ladies. True, ladyhood offers tremendous social advantages: the ability not to offend one's fellow man, by employing kindness and empathy, is hardly reprehensible. But it can kill a writer's voice. Dead. Ladyhood comes with stern voices warning against use of our personal material. At all costs, we must keep the family secrets. Be loyal. Make sure nobody is hurt or offended by what we say. Put on our best face. Control our image. Write glowing thank you notes even when we had a rotten time. And never, never wear unsightly underwear, lest the emergency room orderly be offended and/ or speak ill of our family. A little smile broke across Cheryl's face.

Suddenly inspired, I issued the class a homework challenge: everyone was to write about something that terrified or embarrassed them — something they'd rather others not know. This they would read aloud — with the understanding that everything revealed would "stay in the room." Trust would be essential.

Cheryl didn't volunteer to read first. As others poured out their fearsome material, it became clear that one man's shame is another's lollipop. Nobody's secrets were any big deal to anyone else. Finally it was Cheryl's turn. She rose. . . and, unflinchingly, read her touching revelation of her bouts with breast cancer.

The class sat in awed silence. More than anyone else, she had given her all. It seems the nutritional value of Truth cannot be underestimated. We all hunger for it. Cheryl had given us a full meal by looking Woman's Worst Fear dead in the eye. Her courage set the tone for the rest of the class. And made me consider anew the areas in which I, after thirty years as a professional writer, still try to protect my secrets . . . to control my image . . . or fail to step forward in the service of Truth. With characteristic courage, Cheryl had stepped forward — the first in the class to write a short story, which became the basis of this book.

Though fictionalized, One Centimeter, sparkles with Truth. It leads us into dark, frightening territory, all the while comforting and consoling us. Through Cheryl's loving eyes, Life becomes a patchwork quilt of little moments to cherish — a quilt to wrap snuggly around ourselves in adversity.

I thank Cheryl for gifting me with many wonderful insights. (For the life of me, I can't remember which of us was supposed to be the instructor.)

Casey Kelly
June 1999

ACKNOWLEDGMENTS

First and foremost, I owe an extraordinary debt to my husband Philip for his unwavering support and vision in recognizing the possibility of these stories in book form, and always for his love. In addition, this book could not have been realized without designer Aimée Bernard de Rubio, whose creative energy, professionalism, and friendship helped create the uniqueness and beauty of the book itself; George Rodrigue, my cousin and lifelong friend, whose generous gift of his artwork graces the cover and brightens the text; John Wilson, my publisher, who has never been anything other than gracious in his support; and Betsy Holden, whose heart was always in the right place as she tirelessly typed this manuscript with skill and dedication.

The arduous task of writing and rewriting could not have been accomplished without the ongoing support of the Cottage Writers Group. I am grateful to Casey Kelly, our fearless leader and teacher, who refused to let me doubt myself. She continually inspires. I feel especially indebted to Candace Marquez and Elizabeth Stein for their writing and editing skills and for their advice on every phase of this project. I also thank Diana Garcia, Scott Wagner, and Ken Zimmern for their encouragement and suggestions on the manuscript.

Jean Wattigny's understanding of south Louisiana culture was invaluable to me, as were her innate literary judgment and astute editing skills. Her wise counsel will long be remembered, for it kept me afloat.

Special thanks go to Jacqueline Simon, whose instructive classes at Rice University's School of Continuing Studies gave birth to these stories, and to Jo-Ann Hungerford for her initial encouragement and work so graciously done on the Two-MaMie photograph. Sally Dooley's distinctive insight into the manuscript was both appreciated and enlightening.

The many kind-hearted health-care professionals I have encountered continue to have my gratitude, especially Dr. Kelly Hunt of M.D. Anderson Cancer Center, whose skills as a surgeon and compassion as a human being know no bounds.

I am forever grateful for my family, especially my eighty-two-year-old mother Irene LeBlanc Courrégé, always the source of my inspiration, for her vivid retelling of stories, and for her encouragement in helping me to remember. I am indebted to my brother John Edward Courrégé for the memories; my sister Susan Phillips, who now shares with me the life-altering experience of being a breast cancer survivor; and my youngest sister Catherine Huckaby, whose discriminating and intuitive comments on the manuscript were especially helpful. Their support and love mean everything to me. And finally, I thank my children, Emily and Martial, not only for their heartening words and Emily's knowledge of the French language, but most of all for being there for me when I needed them most.

What is life?
It is the flash of a firefly in the night.
It is the breath of a buffalo in the wintertime.
It is the little shadow which runs across the grass
and loses itself in the sunset.

CROWFOOT

One Centimeter

"Mrs. Beaulieu, this is Jill at Dr. Hoffman's office. It looks like you'll have to come in for more pictures of your left breast. There appears to be a lesion."

The packages cradled in Anne Beaulieu's arm drop to the floor. "What do you mean a lesion? Don't you mean a lump or a mass? I've never heard it referred to as a lesion before. Didn't Dr. Hoffman just give me a clean bill of health? Does he know about this?"

"Yes, he knows."

"He didn't mention it when I was in two weeks ago." Anne's voice, tightening with tension, rises then falls to just above a whisper. "Why didn't he say something? He had the report then."

"Dr. Hoffman didn't notice until he put it on the hard drive. It's a one-centimeter lesion. I'll have to call you back with the time for the test. I need to call scheduling."

Anne tries to respond, but a wave of nausea floats up her throat, nausea so pronounced her ears begin ringing, forcing her to sit. *Who is this telling me about a lesion on a hard drive?* Pulling the neck of her white turtleneck to give herself more room to breathe, Anne asks, "Please, could you wait forty-five minutes before calling me back? Please? I was just coming in when the phone rang. I need to walk my dog."

Light-headed, her heart now beating violently against her rib cage, Anne slowly puts the receiver down. At her feet lie new linens just purchased at the January sales — down pillows poking out of bags, cotton sheets covering the hardwood floor. Catching her breath, she glances around the kitchen. Her eyes momentarily rest on a long-cased, oak regulator clock, allowing her, for a brief moment, to blank out what she just heard. Out of the silence four melodious bells chime, startling her.

Grabbing the corner of the breakfast trestle table, she steadies herself as she walks over to her

Labrador's bed. Noticing a quizzical expression on Barnaby's face, she bends down and gently nuzzles her head against his. Barnaby's cold nose, soft ears, and his gentle licks on her face calm and soothe her for several minutes. With her anxiety lessened, she grabs Barnaby's lead. Barnaby, reassured too, is up with tail wagging, body shimmying, ready for his walk.

Anne steps out the French doors into the wintry day. The chilly air feels good on her warm, flushed face. At least one thing remains certain: Barnaby likes these cold, cloudy days. Black coat glistening, his body pulls the lead forward. Anne walks briskly, her mind pulsating with conflicting thoughts.

This can't be happening again. Oh God, not again.

Her step quickens. *Dr. Hoffman just checked that same breast two months ago when Paul thought he felt something. And there was nothing there.* She, too, had felt nothing there, certainly nothing different from what she felt in her other breast. After all, it was just two nights ago when Paul told her she looked radiant. *Can you believe? Radiant, bloody radiant!*

Confusion and anger swell within her. *Is it possible to feel so healthy and to have this happen again?* It has been six years since Anne's first diagnosis of breast cancer, six years since she first felt that hard moveable lump in the upper quadrant of her left breast. Heeding the recommendations of her doctors not to have a mastectomy, she had a lumpectomy with lymph node dissection, followed by six weeks of radiation. With no lymph node involvement, she had a good prognosis. Her life quickly returned to the satisfying hum of normalcy, with her daughter Elizabeth's graduation from high school and her son Marc's from eighth grade. Much of her energy was going into Paul's latest business venture when, at her routine two-year checkup, a red flag appeared on the mammogram: a previously undetected group of calcifications in the right breast. A lumpectomy identified the suspicious area as zero-stage breast cancer. This second diagnosis, although in reality less serious than the first, made Anne's mortality seem all the more real. Six weeks of radiation followed, this time on the right breast.

The sun begins to break through the clouds as Anne makes the turn toward home. In this old neighborhood the streets are wide and quiet, the yards broad. She lets Barnaby off his lead to sniff and run as he pleases. Barnaby returns with a ball, not the usual soggy tennis ball, but a brand new baseball. Knowing the home it belongs to, she loosens it from Barnaby's mouth and runs to place it in her neighbor's dense hedge of Indian Hawthorn. Her thoughts are still unrelenting. *How can there be a malignancy in a breast that has been radiated? The radiation must offer some protection.*

However, her logical side knows "it" can come back. She also knows that if "it" has to come back, the breast is the best place for it to be. If there, it is most likely a new occurrence, not a spread or metastasis of the cancer.

Nevertheless, she does not want to get ahead of herself. She doesn't really know if this lesion is malignant. This time she might be one of the lucky ones.

With the adrenaline moving her faster, the three-mile walk, which usually takes forty-five minutes, is done in just under forty. Feeling strengthened, she stops, reaches down, and plucks weeds from the jasmine ground cover in her front garden bed. As she opens the gate to enter her backyard, her head feels clearer, her thoughts more logical.

As promised, Dr. Hoffman's nurse calls back. Anne is to go to the hospital at nine o'clock the following morning.

Anne's husband, Paul, clearing his schedule of his day's commitments, goes with her to the large medical complex. She knows she is fortunate to live near a world-class cancer center, but that knowledge does not abate the queasiness she always feels in the pit of her stomach on test days there.

Anne's first stop is the mammography department, where she immediately recognizes the technician, Bonnie. Although, in some ways, it is comforting to see her, these are not the people she wants to know on a first-name basis. Bonnie is solicitous but acts too cheery, avoiding eye contact. She images Anne's breast four times, compressing the tissue as tightly as she can between the cold plates, so as to get the best pictures. "We need to get the view from all angles, in case surgery is required," Bonnie says.

Trying not to let Bonnie's words disturb her, Anne dresses and rejoins Paul. Together they go by elevator to another large waiting area, where Anne is called into the ultrasound department. When she enters the darkened area, she is surprised to see a nurse standing there waiting to see her. The nurse introduces herself as Jill, Jill from the previous day's telephone call. The waif-like nurse seems too small to be delivering the message she gives Anne.

"There is a small mass in the left breast, about one centimeter. It is near the nipple, in the twelve o'clock position. A technician will ultrasound it, then Dr. Parik will do a needle biopsy."

Jill continues, "Here is the changing room. Take everything off, from the waist up. Remember, the gown ties in front. There is an extra robe to put on in case you get cold."

Once again, Anne removes her black knit sweater. She hangs her lacy bra on the hook provided and loosens the soft leather belt that cinches her small waist. Anne feels relieved she remembered to wear her most comfortable slacks, the ones that feel like silk but are really rayon, the ones she always tries to wear on test days.

As she makes her way into the hall, she sees in the room next to hers a woman lying on a metal bed. Anne pauses for a few seconds, trying to make eye contact, but the woman's expressionless face is turned to one side; she is covered with a blanket.

Anne enters her cold, dark room. All that is visible is a metal bed, a metal table holding the medical supplies, and an ultrasound machine. At least the ultrasound is not intimidating like so many of the other machines she has encountered. Anne edges up onto the metal bed, only lying down when the technician begins to rub her left breast with the cold, gooey gel. She tries to quiet her mind . . .

She is in the pasture behind her childhood home in Louisiana, the live oaks forming a canopy of shade . . .

and, in the middle of the pasture, amidst the many oaks, stands the biggest oak of all, a tree so big that six children holding hands are not able to make a closed circle around it. It is Anne's tree: the one she found on that summer morning so long ago, the tree that she goes to now. Someone has nailed wooden steps up the trunk, making it easier to climb, and between two of its largest branches a small wooden floor has been fashioned. Anne is in that tree, feeling free and uninhibited, a part of the nature that encircles her.

A large, solemn man breaks Anne's reverie. Dr. Parik, the radiologist, looks at the ultrasound screen. He never looks at Anne, only the screen.

"Dr. Parik, do you think it is malignant?"

"Yes."

Anne sits up with a quickness that surprises Dr. Parik. "Well, if you think it is malignant, don't touch it. I don't want malignant cells disturbed with a needle. I want a surgical procedure rather than a needle biopsy."

With no real attempt at pronouncing Beaulieu, Dr. Parik responds, "Mrs. Blue, this is a very safe procedure. I do it at least ten times a day. It is the best course of action to take for many reasons."

As Dr. Parik systematically recites the numerous reasons, Anne relents. She once again lies down and closes her eyes as he plunges the needle once, then twice, into the one-centimeter mass . . .

Anne is back in her tree. This time she has put moss on the small wooden floor, moss that she has pulled like taffy to shake out its loose dirt. On the bed of moss she places a doll's quilt, a quilt made of satin — purple on one side, cream on the other. Lying her head on the satin quilt creates a sensation of coolness and softness that soon encompasses her whole body.

ॐ

The cool, soft sensation continues for Anne as Dr. Parik takes the tissue samples. In doing so, he remarks on the hardness of the mass. Anne's trance is only broken when Dr. Parik puts the samples on four slides and tells her the results will be known in thirty minutes.

Anne, still dressed in her hospital gown, is allowed to go into the waiting area to see Paul. It has been several hours since she has seen him. She finds him talking to a business acquaintance who is undergoing treatment. Paul appears calm, but after twenty-six years of marriage, Anne can read the fear in his expression. She realizes he too, in his own way, is as depleted as she is. Together they prepare for the worst.

Anne is soon called back to the darkened room. Dr. Parik reenters and without a trace of emotion says, "The lab work has come back benign." Seeming angry at the discrepancy between his judgment and the lab results, he repeats in exasperation, "The lab work is benign."

Anne stares at Dr. Parik in disbelief, his tone making her leery of displaying any joy. Irritated, Dr. Parik continues, "The lab work is wrong twenty percent of the time. Now we have no choice. We have to do a core biopsy, where we take bigger samples of the mass."

Before Anne has time to escape back into her other world, Dr. Parik sticks tiny needles into the breast to deaden it. Soon Anne's breast begins to feel like an appendage draping on the table, an appendage no longer a part of her body — it is no longer a vessel of nourishment to sustain new life, no longer a repository of sensuous feelings when gently touched. *It is no longer there.*

Now, with the precision of an engineer, Dr. Parik shoots a bigger needle, which resembles a popgun, into Anne's breast four times. There is no pain in the deadened breast. Dr. Parik tells her it will be three working days before these new test results are known and that Dr. Hoffman will call with the results. Since this is a Wednesday, the wait will actually be five agonizingly long days.

Speaking just above a whisper, Anne asks Dr. Parik, "I don't want to get my hopes up, you know, about the benign report. But isn't that a good sign?"

Still without a trace of emotion Dr. Parik says, "Think of the report as neutral." Then he leaves the room.

Methodically, Anne returns to the dressing area and puts her clothes back on. She tries to make some sense out of the conflicting opinions between Dr. Parik and the lab results. Even if she thinks of the lab report as neutral, she feels it is a positive way to think. Maybe that will be enough to get her through the next few days. When she shares this ray of hope with Paul, she cries her first tears since the telephone call.

Anne and Paul decide to keep as normal a schedule as possible. They do not cancel their planned weekend trip to visit Marc, now in his first year of college. They want to keep Anne's mind occupied and focused on something other than the Monday telephone call.

However, everything she does that weekend has a heightened intensity, a certain poignancy, as when they buy a fleece-lined jacket for their son. It is more than just buying a jacket; it becomes an act of nurturing, one of love and protection, one that she hopes will not only keep Marc's body warm but his spirit as well.

When the weekend draws to a close, Anne feels that old familiar pang in the pit of her stomach. On the four-hour drive home she tells Paul about the recurring dream she has had.

"I'm a child again. The carnival is in town. The sticky, sweet smell of harvested cane is everywhere. I'm with my friends, happy, laughing, waiting in line to ride a merry-go-round. More than anything I want to get on that merry-go-round. I want to stay in line, to be part of the group, when suddenly, out of nowhere, this incredible force pulls me aside and a voice says, 'We are going to stay here for awhile. You are not to go with the others.' Oh, Paul, I am so frightened."

Thunder awakens Anne on Monday morning. The predicted arctic cold front is quickly moving in. She gets out of bed, her head heavy from a sleeping pill. Looking out of the frosted panes of glass, she can almost feel the bitter cold she knows will soon be here. Normally, she loves these freezing winter days, that are rare where she lives. However, this day is different. She hopes the weather is not an ominous sign while she kneels by the side of her bed and prays, *Dear God, give me the grace and courage to face this day, to accept the news if it is not good.*

Anne goes down to breakfast with Paul. Tolerating only tea and toast, she doesn't want to hear sounds from the stereo or television. She tries to read the newspaper, finds it difficult to concentrate, and returns upstairs. The morning is unending.

Paul goes to his office, but knowing Dr. Hoffman makes his phone calls in the afternoon, he returns before lunch. Before entering the house, he gathers firewood from the stack on the back porch. Once inside, he quickly lights two fires, one in the kitchen, the other in the living room. Rubbing his cold, wet hands together he looks at Anne a long time before he says, "These old houses don't keep us warm, do they?"

Before Anne can respond, she sees their daughter Elizabeth pulling up in the long driveway. Anne gives thanks that, at least temporarily, their daughter, whose college years were spent on the East Coast, lives near them. As Anne opens the door to greet her, she hears the tapping sound of Elizabeth's shoes on the outside brick pavers. Elizabeth, bundled up, brow furrowed, walks rapidly toward her mother. She carries a bag of sandwiches. Anne attempts to speak but cannot; all she can do is throw her arms around her daughter's neck.

After lunch, quiet descends on the house. There isn't much to say. Anne feels numb, desensitized. The air hangs heavy with anxiety, making her wish she could run away. Paul reaches for her hand and they go with Elizabeth into the living room, where the fire is now blazing. Barnaby follows close behind; he positions himself near the sofa where his family now waits.

The phone call comes just after three o'clock. The ring shatters the still air.

"Dr. Hoffman here. How are you, Anne?" It is a perfunctory courtesy; Dr. Hoffman doesn't really expect an answer. The pause seems eternal.

"Anne, it is malignant. The reason the initial lab results were benign is that it appears to have good differentiation."

Anne lets out a pained little gasp. Her throat tightens and becomes increasingly dry as she asks Dr. Hoffman questions. Somehow, she is still able to focus on his answers: "Yes, the estrogen receptor test is positive. No, the lesion is not *in situ*. It is invasive ductal carcinoma."

Finally, when they talk about what would be the best treatment option for the one-centimeter lesion, Anne's head begins to spin. She has no doubt what Dr. Hoffman will recommend, for as he told her once before in his athletic lingo, "If it ever happens again, it's a slam dunk." Deep inside, Anne has always known too, what she would do if another breast malignancy appeared. To her it has always been a foregone conclusion that she would have a double mastectomy. However, every fibre of her being revolts that it has come down to this: something as small as a one-centimeter lesion, even with its life-threatening potential, is propelling her in a direction that at one time she never thought possible. In order to be whole again, she must lose part of her physical self.

When Anne finally puts the receiver down, she sees Paul and Elizabeth, tears brimming in their eyes. They walk over to her. Anne stands up in an almost dazed state, her legs now wobbly.

"Paul, it has good differentiation, good differentiation, Paul, that is important, don't you understand, good differentiation." Paul whispers, "It's going to be all right," as his arms encircle Anne and then include Elizabeth. The sobs begin to come as Anne buries her head in Paul's chest.

TWO-MAMIE

Two-MaMie was nicknamed by my older brother, John Edward. Upon hearing our Mama calling her mother "Mama," John Edward, at a young age, thought he had two mamas. No name could have been more appropriate.

Two-MaMie is the only grandparent I remember. Standing five-foot-four, her medium-boned frame was crowned with long, dark hair, which she always wore in a bun, pinned low at the nape of her neck. Freckled arms, a large bosom, and an equally large lap all came together to form a presence I could not ignore.

Born in 1882 in a small south Louisiana town, Two-MaMie was true to her heritage. Although her family had been here for at least two generations, her accent gave away the fact that French was her first language. Forbidden to speak it in school, French still remained her favorite way of expressing herself, as if it were in her bones and soul.

The summer I was turning five, Two-MaMie came to visit often. She would travel the twenty miles with her son, my *parrain* or godfather, to be with us. Her mission that summer of 1949 was to help Mama, who was expecting her third baby in the fall. Because Mama was worried our French heritage was being lost forever, she was also to become my unofficial French teacher. However, I suspect the lessons were done in an attempt to please and reassure me, because of the new baby.

During the times we practiced French, our screened-in front porch served as the classroom, where a ceiling fan kept air flowing on those hot, steamy days. Two-MaMie would choose her favorite comfortable rocker and up I would climb into her lap. *Un, deux, trois, quatre, cinq* . . . The combination of the rocking and the rhythm of the language had a stilling effect on me. So, when Two-MaMie would point to my ear, nose, and mouth, I would respond with as much seriousness as I could muster: *l'oreille, le nez, and la bouche.* She always called me *ma p'tite Chérie* or sometimes just *p'tite*.

The high point of the summer of '49 was my fifth birthday party. Again, anxious to show me favor, Mama and Papa decided to give me a party I wouldn't be likely to forget. Twenty-five invitations went out to family and friends stating "Pony Rides For Everyone!" The pony they intended to use was John Edward's. Since it was frisky and larger than most ponies, Papa himself planned to lead the pony around in a large circle in the front yard.

Assisting with the preparations, I helped Mama make little paper-basket party favors that would hold jellybeans and silver bells. I even helped decorate the three-layered cake with white mountain frosting, sprinkling coconut on top. When, at long last, the afternoon of the party arrived, I couldn't help being in a state of mild euphoria. I thought the front yard looked like the grounds of a circus. The shiny brown-and-white pony, all saddled up, stood ready to carry children on his back. The swing set, washed and gleaming, awaited the aspiring trapeze artists. And, in the center of the lawn, stood our young oak tree, decorated with balloons. It seemed to touch the clouds.

Coming from her home, Two-MaMie arrived after the party started. I could see her limping up the driveway. Before this important day, Two-MaMie had always seemed indestructible.

Running to greet her I asked, "Two MaMie what's wrong? You're late. I was so worried."

"Oh, nothing *p'tite*. I think I just stumbled on a rock."

Despite what she said, I could tell she wasn't feeling well; beads of sweat were on her forehead. Nevertheless, I saw Two-MaMie's spirits lift when she noticed what was taking place on the front lawn. Mama and I helped her onto the front porch. There, she could comfortably watch John Edward supervising the trapeze artists and Papa helping the children get onto the pony. She could also keep a careful eye on a big willow basket that was already overflowing with gaily covered packages. In fact, Mama appointed Two-MaMie guardian of the gifts, since I had been eyeing the basket for quite some time. For sure, I had never seen so many boxes with pretty papers and bright ribbons in my young life. And I suppose neither had Two-MaMie.

Time and time again, I would leave the party and sneak up on the porch, professing to see how Two-MaMie was feeling, but really wanting to check on the gifts.

"Two-MaMie, what do you think? Have you ever seen so many presents?"

"Goodness no. Ah so many, *ma p'tite Chèrie.*"

"They are so beautiful. Can I open one, please, just one?"

"Oh, one won't matter. Of course you can, *p'tite*."

It was then that Two-MaMie and I became coconspirators. Two-MaMie moved closer to the basket, her eyes growing brighter as I unwrapped that first gift. When I saw the tiny blue-and-white porcelain tea set, I gasped, "Oh Two-MaMie. This is what I've always wanted. It's from *Parrain*."

After that it was not hard to convince her I should open another gift, then another. I worked quickly until all were open.

When the realization of what we were doing hit Two-MaMie, she let out a long sigh, "Oh *Mon Dieu*, Anne! My Lord! What will we tell your parents? You must go back to your friends now. Don't worry, I'll put everything back in the basket. Now, run along."

I gaped at all the torn paper and the basket overflowing with wind-up toys, stuffed animals, and God knows what. Leaving the scene, I observed Two-MaMie trying to rewrap the gifts. Rejoining the party, I felt excited and guilty all at the same time. Guilty for leaving Two-MaMie with such a huge task.

I was lucky the party moved along so quickly because there was never time for my friends to watch me open the gifts. I was luckier still that my parents had a good sense of humor. When all the guests had left and Mama and Papa decided it was now *the time* to open the presents, their jaws dropped open when they saw a basket brimming with gifts — all wrapped with torn paper and bedraggled bows. As for Two-MaMie and me, we let out a sigh of relief when we saw Mama's and Papa's worried looks turn into little smiles and then deepen into wide grins.

Weeks after the celebration of my fifth birthday, Two-MaMie continued to feel tired and just not herself. Because of Mama's refusal to take "no" for an answer, Two-MaMie finally agreed to take a medical exam. The results astonished us: Two-MaMie had paratyphoid fever. Although a milder form of typhoid fever, it still has many of the same symptoms: stomach inflammation and hot sweats. It is also — infectious!

Although I was beside myself with worry about Two-MaMie, I thought it to be an exciting time. She would stay with us for a whole month to recover. Mama and Papa took precautions to ensure the disease would not spread. John Edward and I moved out of our shared bedroom so she could move in. With enthusiasm and haste, we placed all of our things in the living room. My father placed Two-MaMie's bed in the center of our room, and in place of the doors, my mother hung white sheer curtains so we could visit her without ever entering the room. The doctor ordered complete bed rest and medicine — at least ten pills a day! He also ordered typhoid shots for the whole family.

After Two-MaMie was comfortably set up in her room, arrangements were made for us to get our shots. We went to the doctor's office in shifts so Two-MaMie was never left unattended. Since he had to go to work, my father was first; Mama and John Edward were next. It happened so fast, before I had time to think, I was in charge of Two-MaMie.

I peered through the curtains to check on her. A fan was whirring; the windows were open. Two-MaMie was in bed with her head propped up, her hair falling softly on the pillow.

"I'm fine Anne. You don't have to stay by the curtains and watch me. Besides, your Mama will be home in thirty minutes. Go and see if Baby George can play with you."

"Are you sure, Two-MaMie?"

"*Ma p'tite Chèrie*, I'm positive. You go now."

I was soon out of the house looking for Baby George. He was not a baby; it was just that his daddy was Big George or Uncle George. Not only was Baby George my cousin, he was my best friend. He lived right next door in a red brick duplex apartment his father had built.

I knocked on the front door of the brick duplex. No one was home. I paced up and down the concrete porch. Finally, I looked up and saw the ropes of a green cloth awning. So I naturally thought, "Ah, perfect for practicing my balancing. I can walk on the windowsill."

The windowsill was half as tall as I was. I backed up, made a few running steps and jumped onto the slanted concrete, grabbing the awning rope for support. I walked on the ledge, trying to be as careful as I could be, putting one foot in front of the other. At the same time my arms began stretching backwards. At the last minute, I realized the rope wasn't moving with me. I had to let go! In an instant, I was on the concrete — head first.

"Oh God, it hurts." Tears stung my eyes. "Where in the world is Baby George? Where's his Mama?

Aunt Marie!" I had no choice. I had to run home to Two-MaMie.

I rushed through the curtains right into her room.

"*Mon Dieu*, Anne! What happened to you? Look at your head, *pauvre 'tite bébé*! Poor little baby!"

I lifted my hand and felt a huge bump on my head. I ran to the bathroom mirror. The bump was the size of a goose egg and it was growing! Only this goose egg was yellow and purple.

Before I knew it, Two-MaMie was out of bed and in the kitchen opening the refrigerator. She told me to go and sit on the sofa. By this time, I was sobbing. Two-MaMie took long, slow steps. She came and sat next to me on the sofa, holding cold butter and a silver butter knife. I was bewildered. She looked at my goose egg, lifted the knife with butter on it and started spreading the butter on my forehead. It didn't spread well, so she sat there trying to keep the butter on the goose egg with the knife.

At that moment, Mama entered, stunned. First to see Two-MaMie in the living room, then to see me, the left side of my forehead protruding out with butter spread on it. Two-MaMie looked up help-less.

"What could I do, Irene? You had better take her to the doctor right now."

Mama put her mother back to bed and washed the butter off me. Then she immediately took me to the doctor. To everyone's relief, I was fine and so was Two-MaMie. She continued her recovery, and I didn't get paratyphoid fever.

TWO-MAMIE EPILOGUE

Mama's birthday blends into the Christmas preparations. She doesn't seem to mind. Humming "Silent Night," she pours anisette into crystal bottles; into one she pours red, into the other green. She made the rich concoction of sugar, water, alcohol, and anisette flavoring, bought at Taylor's Drug Store, several days ago. As Mama pours, the anisette glistens in the decanters. Sitting there on the sideboard, the crystal bottles sparkle like jewels. With their deep colors of red and green, they are a decoration unto themselves. Mama finally pours green anisette into a tiny glass for me to taste. My lips pucker — it tastes like sweet licorice. It is Christmas Eve and Mama's thirty-second birthday.

Two-MaMie, now returned to her good health from the paratyphoid fever, arrives early to spend the day with us. Wearing a deep green dress that shows off her new figure, Two-MaMie doesn't waste any time, going directly to the kitchen to begin cutting onions and celery for tomorrow's rice dressing. She slices cold boiled yams that Mama will soon turn into something resembling candy.

With so much going on, Mama calls me to watch my new baby sister, Mary Susan, who is fussing. I sit and rock the bassinet while listening to the Christmas carols. Honestly, I can sit here all day and listen to those carols, especially Bing Crosby singing about a white Christmas. After all, he is Two-MaMie's favorite singer. Before we know it, it's four o'clock and *Parrain* is here to take Two-MaMie home. But, I explain to *Parrain*: "Don't leave yet. We have to exchange our gifts with Two-MaMie. Don't you know, we always do family gifts on Christmas Eve."

I can't wait to open Two-MaMie's gift to me. I know she is making a quilt for the doll that Santa is bringing. Two-MaMie makes the most beautiful quilts, from tiny scraps of material; some of the scraps are even from my dresses. I am hoping my doll's quilt will be creamy pastels, a patchwork one, but when I open my gift I see a shiny, puffy satin quilt — purple on one side, cream on the other. Too surprised, I don't say anything. However, Two-MaMie can tell something's wrong.

"*P'tite*, Santa is bringing you a very pretty doll. This is something beautiful for her. Look, I even made a pillow to match the quilt."

"Oh, Two-MaMie, I like the quilt. It is just different from what I thought you were making." I quickly turn away and say, "Oh, now it's time to open your gift."

Two-MaMie smiles when she lifts out of a velvet box a large, blue crystal rosary with a silver cross.

"Two-MaMie on the back of the cross, look. It's your name."

Two-MaMie's eyes cloud over when she reads: Ezilda D. Bodin, December 25, 1949. She reaches over and hugs me. Then, Two-MaMie gathers her things since she wants to be home before dark. I kiss her and *Parrain* goodbye. Mama kisses them too and adds a warning to be careful on the road and not be late tomorrow for our Christmas celebration.

The house slips into a silence while Mama prepares a special omelet for our supper. Papa, John Edward, and I sit around the kitchen table waiting to taste this new dish, when the phone rings. Mama goes to the hall to answer it. She doesn't say anything for a long time and then begins asking lots of questions. We know something is wrong by the way she is talking. No one touches the omelet.

Standing there, with no color left in her face, Mama tells us: "It's Two-MaMie. She's hurt. I don't know how serious. She's alive and on her way to the hospital." We all stare at Mama, as she continues, "Two-MaMie was struck by a car while crossing the street. She was going to show Mrs. Krepper her new rosary," Mama takes a deep breath, "and to ask her to go to midnight Mass. They are taking her to Dauterive Hospital. I need to go."

Hearing such news, I feel like I might suffocate. I run to the bathroom gagging. "How can Two-MaMie be hurt? She was just here."

The house seems all a mess now. Papa clears the uneaten dinner as Mama gets ready to leave. We all try our best to help.

Mama grabs her coat and gets into our new '49 Ford. She turns the ignition, puts her foot on the pedal and nothing happens . . . nothing happens. I keep running to the back door, looking at the garage and the sky full of stars and beg, "Please God, let the car start. Mama needs to get to Two-MaMie. Please, let Two-MaMie be all right."

Thank God, Uncle George comes over to help. He brings his jumper cables; he jump-starts the car and Mama is off.

Now the phone rings non-stop. Papa speaks in a soft, low voice and makes phone calls himself. He says, "Aunt Bert is coming to stay with you." Leaving, he tells us to be good and go to sleep. John Edward and I kneel by our beds and say prayers for Two-MaMie.

I feel tired, so very tired I fall asleep.

Christmas morning. The tree lights are still on, sparkling through the mass of silver icicles. I see a baby buggy under the tree. Looking inside, I find the most beautiful baby doll, her head resting on a satin pillow. I notice Santa has even covered her with the purple quilt Two-MaMie made.

I run to Mama's and Papa's room to tell them what Santa has left for me. They're not there; John Edward is not around, either. I hear voices in the kitchen. Everyone is in there, talking softly. I look around and see tears in Mama's eyes. Mama gets up to hug me. I know something dreadful has happened. No one has to tell me. Two-MaMie is dead.

I am weak, confused. It's like a rock is pounding me, squeezing out all of my happiness.

Mama and Papa plan the funeral and Mama explains: "Anne, you're only five. You might have sad memories about Two-MaMie if you come. I want you to remember her as she was, strong and happy, and full of love for you."

"But, Mama, John Edward is going to the funeral."

"John Edward is four years older than you, Anne. I hope one day you'll understand."

I am frightened and fearful of death, but I want to be with my family and with Two-MaMie. I want to tell her goodbye. Also, I know Two-MaMie would want me at her funeral because, just a few weeks before, she asked Mama if she could take me to Great Aunt Lillie's funeral. Mama smiled when she told me, "Anne, she just wants to show you off to her friends."

So, I don't go to the funeral. I wait at home with the lady hired to take care of Mary Susan and me. When my family returns, everyone is very quiet. Mama has a look I have not seen before. She looks so sad, yet at the same time strong. She looks taller; maybe it is just the black dress and the heels or maybe it is her new strength. She sits next to me and says, "Anne, Two-MaMie was so loved. The church was overflowing with people." I can barely look at Mama's eyes, her hurt seems so great.

Several days after the funeral, Mama and I drive the twenty miles to Two-MaMie's house. I walk up the high steps and stand on her large front porch. Mama goes inside to begin clearing out her things. I don't want to go inside. Instead, I climb into a rocker and think. I think about lots of things. I think about my new little sister — I have to help Mama take care of her now. I think about Two-MaMie crossing the street to show Mrs. Krepper her rosary. I look across the street at Mrs. Krepper's house a long, long time. I imagine Two-MaMie making it to the other side. I see Two-MaMie's smile, and I feel her arms around me.